Emall
LEN

Lenski, Lois.

I like winter.

W9-APX-779

$11.99   01-C428

DATE			

Copyright © 1950 by Lois Lenski.
All rights reserved under International and Pan-American Copyright
Conventions. Published in the United States by Random House, Inc., New York, and
simultaneously in Canada by Random House of Canada Limited, Toronto.
Originally published by Oxford University Press in 1950.
www.randomhouse.com/kids
ISBN: 0-375-81068-4
Library of Congress Catalog Card Number: 00-100898
Printed in the United States of America   October 2000   10 9 8 7 6 5 4 3 2 1
RANDOM HOUSE and colophon are registered trademarks of Random House, Inc.

I LIKE WINTER

LOIS LENSKI

Random House 🏠 New York

I LIKE WINTER

WORDS AND MELODY BY LOIS LENSKI
ARRANGEMENT BY CLYDE ROBERT BULLA

I like win-ter, I like snow. I like i-cy winds that blow. I like snow-flakes, oh, so light

mak-ing all the ground so white. I like slid-ing down the hill, I like tumb-ling in a spill.

CHORUS

Oh, ho! seas-ons come and seas-ons go. I like win-ter, I like snow.

I like winter, I like snow.
I like icy winds that blow.
I like snowflakes, oh so light,
Making all the ground so white.

I like sliding down the hill,
I like tumbling
                    in
                        a
                            spill!

I can make a snowman fat,
Eyes and nose and funny hat.

I can squeeze a snowball tight.
Throw it in a
    snowball fight.

I can skate and slip and slide—
Ice is thick, the pond is wide.

My feet get cold,
    my poor hands freeze,
        I'm catching cold,
            I shiver and sneeze—
                (Ker-chooo!)

And then I have to stay in bed,
Because I have a stuffed-up head.

The wind blows hard
    and piles up snow—
I'm up again
        and out I go.

I like Christmas—dark green tree,
Colored lights for all to see.

I like candles shining bright
In the window when it's night.

I like wreaths of pretty green,
Hung up high so they'll be seen.

I like stockings in a row—
Stockings empty to the toe.

I like Santa
      with a sack
Full of toys
      upon his back.

I like people

who come to stay—

I like lights that shine for me,
Brightly on the Christmas tree.

Baby Jesus, born today;
See Him sleeping on the hay.

On His birthday, let us sing
Christmas carols to our King.

I like gifts around the tree,
Oh, what fun for you and me!

I like presents—yes, I do!
But I like to give them, too.

I like winter—long it stays,
Long the nights and short the days.

Comes a morning bright and fine,
When I make a Valentine.

Flowers pretty, heart of red;
"I love you!" That's what it said.

Summer, winter, spring, or fall—
I love *you* the best of all.